This book belongs to

____

Hansel and Gretel

BY

The Brothers Grimm

Retold by Fiona Black

ILLUSTRATED BY

John Gurney

ARIEL BOOKS

ANDREWS AND McMEEL

KANSAS CITY

 For information write Andrews and McMeel, a Universal Press Syndicate Company, 4900 Main Street, Kansas City, Missouri 64112.

Library of Congress Cataloging-in-Publication Data

Grimm, Jacob, 1785–1863.
[Hänsel und Gretel. English]
Hansel and Gretel / the brothers Grimm ; retold by Fiona Black ; illustrated by John Gurney.
p. cm.
Translation of: Hänsel und Gretel.
Summary: A poor woodcutter's two children, lost in the woods, come upon a gingerbread house inhabited by a wicked witch.
ISBN 0-8362-4912-7 : $6.95
[1. Fairy tales. 2. Folklore—Germany.] I. Grimm, Wilhelm, 1786–1859. II. Black, Fiona. III. Gurney, John, ill. IV. Title.
PZ8.G882Han 1991
398.2—dc20 91-10100
[E] CIP
AC

Design: Susan Hood and Mike Hortens
Art Direction: Armand Eisen, Mike Hortens, and Julie Phillips
Art Production: Lynn Wine
Production: Julie Miller and Lisa Shadid

Hansel and Gretel

In a small cottage at the edge of a large forest, there once lived a poor woodcutter with his second wife. Now this woodcutter had two children from his first marriage, a boy named Hansel and a girl named Gretel.

Little by little, the woodcutter became poorer and poorer, until finally he did not have even enough money for food.

One night, the woodcutter said to his wife, "What are we to do? We cannot feed our children or ourselves."

"There is only one thing to do," his wife replied. "We will give each of the children one last piece of bread. Then we must take them into the forest and leave them there. They can find their own food."

"I cannot do that to my own children!" the woodcutter cried. "They will die in the woods." But his wife nagged him until he agreed with her plan.

Hansel and Gretel were awake and they overheard their stepmother's words. Gretel began to cry. "Don't be afraid," her brother said. "I am sure I can think of a way to save us."

After his parents were asleep, Hansel crept out of the house. In the garden, the moon shone brightly on the white pebbles, making them gleam like silver.

Hansel filled his pockets with pebbles and went back inside. "Sleep in peace, dear Gretel," he said. "All will be well."

Early the next morning, their stepmother shook them awake. "Get up! We are going into the forest to chop wood," she said. "Here is a piece of bread for your lunch. But don't eat it until then, for it's all you'll get!"

Gretel hid Hansel's piece of bread in her apron pocket, as Hansel's pockets were full of pebbles. Then they all started out into the forest.

Along the way Hansel kept turning and looking back at the cottage. "Come along," his father scolded. "Why are you dallying?"

"Oh," Hansel replied. "I am only saying good-bye to my white kitten who is sitting on the roof."

"Don't be silly!" said his stepmother. "That is not your kitten. That's only the sun shining on the roof."

But Hansel was not really saying good-bye to his kitten. Each time he turned he dropped a white pebble on the path.

When they reached the middle of the forest, Hansel's father and stepmother made a big fire. "Stay here by the warm fire and eat your lunch, children," their stepmother said. "Your father and I are going further into the forest to chop wood."

So Hansel and Gretel sat by the fire and ate their bread. They believed their parents were close by, for they thought they heard the chopping of their father's axe. But it was only the wind knocking a dead branch against a tree.

After a while, the children fell asleep. When they awoke, it was dark and their parents were nowhere to be seen. Gretel began to sob, but Hansel said, "Do not fret, little sister. Wait until the moon rises."

And when the moon rose, Hansel took Gretel's hand and they followed the trail of white pebbles home.

Their father threw his arms around his children, for he was sorry for having left them in the forest. But soon the family was hungry again. One night, Hansel and Gretel heard their stepmother say to their father, "We must get rid of the children! This time we must take them so far into the forest that they will never find their way back!"

When his parents were asleep, Hansel tried to go outside to pick up pebbles. But this time the door was locked.

The next morning, Hansel and Gretel's stepmother gave them each a tiny piece of bread. Then they all set out into the forest.

On the way, Hansel crumbled the bread in his pocket and scattered the crumbs along the path. When his father asked him why he was going so slowly, Hansel replied, "I am only saying good-bye to my pigeon who is cooing on the chimney."

"Don't be silly," his stepmother scolded. "That's not your pigeon. That is only the sun shining on the chimney!"

But Hansel was not really saying good-bye to his pigeon. He was carefully sprinkling crumbs on the path, until all his bread was gone.

This time their parents took Hansel and Gretel to a part of the forest they had never seen before. Then the woodcutter made an even bigger fire. “Eat your bread by the warm fire,” their stepmother said. “We are going to chop wood, and we will return for you when we are finished.”

Gretel shared her piece of bread with her brother. Then the two children grew drowsy and fell asleep.

When they awoke it was night. They called as loudly as they could for their father and stepmother, but no one came. Gretel began to cry, but Hansel said to her, “Wait until the moon rises. Then we will follow the bread crumbs I scattered all the way home.”

But when the moon rose, there were no bread crumbs to be found. The birds of the forest had eaten them all.

"Let us just walk," Hansel said to Gretel. "We will find our way home, you'll see." But they walked all night long and could not find their way out of the forest.

The next day the children walked from dawn to dusk, and still they were lost in the great forest. Nothing they saw looked familiar.

Hansel and Gretel were very hungry, for since finishing their bread, they had eaten nothing except the few nuts they found on the ground. By nightfall, they were too tired and weak to go on any further. They lay down at the foot of a tree and fell asleep.

As soon as Hansel and Gretel awoke the next morning, they began walking. Their hearts were heavy, for they knew that if they did not find a way out of the forest soon, they would surely die there.

Then Hansel and Gretel spotted a beautiful white bird perched on a low branch of a nearby tree. The bird began to sing. Its voice was so sweet that the children stopped to listen. Then the bird flapped its wings and came to fly just ahead of them.

"It is almost as if it were trying to lead us somewhere!" Hansel cried.

The children followed the beautiful white bird through the forest, until it brought them to a little house and alighted on its roof.

When Hansel and Gretel drew closer, they saw that the house was made of gingerbread, with a roof of raisin cake. The windows were made of sugar candy, and the eaves and sills were trimmed with sugar icing.

Hansel turned to his sister and said, "Now we shall have a good meal! I'll eat the roof and you start on the windows!"

Hansel broke off a corner of the roof, while Gretel knocked out a windowpane. But just as they began eating, a gruff voice from inside the house cried:

Crunching and nibbling like a mouse!
Who is eating up my house?

Hansel and Gretel replied:

It is just the wind on high,
Blowing, bumping through the sky!

The children were so hungry they could not stop eating. Hansel tore another piece from the roof. Meanwhile, Gretel pulled off a windowsill and gobbled it down.

Just then the door of the gingerbread house flew open, and out hobbled an old woman with a cane.

Hansel and Gretel were frightened, but the old woman said to them kindly, "Don't be afraid. I won't hurt you. Come in!"

The old woman fed them apple pancakes with sugar and raisins. Then she led them to two snug little beds. Hansel and Gretel fell fast asleep, believing they were safe at last.

But the old woman was not as kind as she seemed. She was really a wicked witch who invited children into her gingerbread house so that she could eat them.

Early the next morning the wicked witch shook Hansel awake. She took him to a dark cell beneath the house and locked him inside.

Then the witch went back upstairs to wake Gretel. "Get up," she cackled. "There is work to do! You must cook food for your brother. I wish to make him nice and fat and then I will eat him up!"

Gretel began to weep, but there was nothing she could do.

Every day Hansel was given plenty of good food—chicken and dumplings, thick stews and biscuits, and rich cakes of all kinds. Poor Gretel was fed only dry crusts of bread.

Every day the witch went to Hansel's cell to see how fat he had become. "Stick out your finger," she said, "and let me see if you are plump yet."

Instead of his finger, clever Hansel stuck out a chicken bone. The witch, who was very nearsighted, would feel the bone and go away grumbling because Hansel was still not fat enough to eat.

The old witch grew impatient. One day she decided not to wait anymore and she began to prepare Hansel for eating.

She called Gretel and said, "I wish to bake some bread. I have made the dough and lit the oven. Just crawl inside and tell me if it is hot enough yet."

The witch meant to close the oven door as soon as Gretel was inside and cook her, too. But Gretel knew what the witch was thinking and asked, "How do I get in?"

"How stupid you are!" replied the witch. "Just crawl in. Watch how I do it." And she stuck her head in the oven.

Quickly Gretel shoved the witch into the oven. Then she shut the door and bolted it.

How the witch screamed! But Gretel paid no attention. She ran and unlocked the door to her brother's cell. "Oh, Hansel!" she cried. "The wicked witch is dead and we can leave this place!" She threw her arms around her brother and they both wept with joy.

Now that the witch was dead, Hansel and Gretel decided to explore the gingerbread house. To their delight, they found chests full of gold and jewels. Hansel stuffed his pockets with the riches, and Gretel filled her apron.

Then the two children walked into the forest. They walked all day. Toward evening, they reached the edge of the forest. They came upon a familiar path with flowers growing along it. "Look, Gretel," cried Hansel. "We're not lost anymore!"

In the distance, the children spotted their father's cottage. They began running toward it. When they burst through the door they found their father sitting alone by the fireplace.

The woodcutter was overjoyed to see his children again. His wife had died, and he had not smiled once since he had left Hansel and Gretel alone in the forest.

The children showed him the gold and jewels they had found in the witch's house. Now, they would all live happily ever after, and never be hungry again.

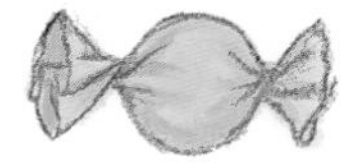

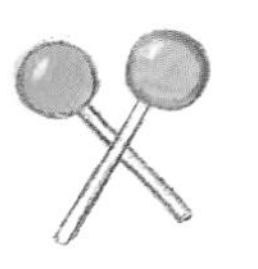

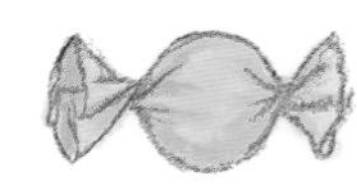